By Neil Gaiman and published by Headline

The View From The Cheap Seats
Trigger Warning
The Ocean at the End of the Lane
Fragile Things
Anansi Boys
American Gods
Stardust
Smoke and Mirrors
Neverwhere

How the Marquis Got His Coat Back
(a Neverwhere *short story)*

Illustrated editions

American Gods
Anansi Boys
The Monarch of the Glen
Black Dog
(illustrated by Daniel Egnéus)

Neverwhere
(illustrated by Chris Riddell)

The Truth is a Cave in the Black Mountains
(illustrated by Eddie Campbell)

How to Talk to Girls at Parties
(adaptation and artwork by Fábio Moon and Gabriel Bá)

Troll Bridge
(Adaptation and artwork by Colleen Doran)

MirrorMask: The Illustrated Film Script
(with Dave McKean)

NEIL GAIMAN
BLACK DOG

ILLUSTRATED BY
DANIEL EGNÉUS

HEADLINE

First published in *Trigger Warning* in Great Britain in 2015 by
HEADLINE PUBLISHING GROUP

First published in *Trigger Warning* in paperback in Great Britain in 2015 by
HEADLINE PUBLISHING GROUP

This edition published in 2016 by
HEADLINE PUBLISHING GROUP

5

ISBN 978 1 4722 3544 2

Typeset in Zapf Elliptical and Priori Serif by Patrick Insole

Printed and bound in Great Britain by Clays Ltd, Elcograf S.p.A.

MIX
Paper from
responsible sources
FSC® C104740

Headline's policy is to use papers that are natural, renewable and recyclable
products and made from wood grown in sustainable forests. The logging and
manufacturing processes are expected to conform to the environmental regulations
of the country of origin.

HEADLINE PUBLISHING GROUP
An Hachette UK Company
Carmelite House
50 Victoria Embankment
London, EC4Y 0DZ

www.headline.co.uk
www.hachette.co.uk

To Colin and Susannah,
for a different night in a similar pub
N. G.

For Eva and Sussi
D. E.

There were ten tongues within one head
And one went out to fetch some bread,
To feed the living and the dead.

Old Riddle

I

THE BAR GUEST

Outside the pub it was raining cats and dogs.

Shadow was still not entirely convinced that he was in a pub. True, there was a tiny bar at the back of the room, with bottles behind it and a couple of the huge taps you pulled, and there were several high tables and people were drinking at the tables, but it all felt like a room in somebody's house. The dogs helped reinforce that impression. It seemed to Shadow that everybody in the pub had a dog except for him.

'What kind of dogs are they?' Shadow asked, curious. The dogs reminded him of greyhounds, but they were smaller and seemed saner, more placid and less high strung than the greyhounds he had encountered over the years.

'Lurchers,' said the pub's landlord, coming out from behind the bar. He was carrying a pint of beer that he had poured for himself. 'Best dogs. Poacher's dogs. Fast, smart, lethal.' He bent down, scratched a chestnut-and-white brindled dog behind the ears. The dog stretched and luxuriated in the ear-scratching. It did not look particularly lethal, and Shadow said so.

The landlord, his hair a mop of grey and orange, scratched at his beard reflectively. 'That's where you'd be wrong,' he said. 'I walked with his brother last week, down Cumpsy Lane. There's a fox, a big red reynard, pokes his head out of a hedge, no more than twenty metres down the road, then, plain as day, saunters out onto the track. Well, Needles sees it, and he's off after it like the clappers. Next thing you know, Needles has his teeth in reynard's neck, and one bite, one hard shake, and it's all over.'

Shadow inspected Needles, a grey dog sleeping by the little fireplace. He looked harmless too. 'So what sort of a breed is a lurcher? It's an English breed, yes?'

'It's not actually a breed,' said a white-haired woman without a dog who had been leaning on a nearby table. 'They're crossbred for speed, stamina. Sighthound, greyhound, collie.'

The man next to her held up a finger. 'You must understand,' he said, cheerfully, 'that there used to be laws about who could own purebred dogs. The local folk couldn't, but they could own mongrels. And lurchers are better and faster than pedigree dogs.' He pushed his spectacles up his nose with the tip of his forefinger. He had a muttonchop beard, brown flecked with white.

'Ask me, all mongrels are better than pedigree anything,' said the woman. 'It's why America is such an interesting country. Filled with mongrels.' Shadow was not certain how old she was. Her hair was white, but she seemed younger than her hair.

'Actually, darling,' said the man with the muttonchops,

in his gentle voice, 'I think you'll find that the Americans are keener on pedigree dogs than the British. I met a woman from the American Kennel Club, and honestly, she scared me. I was scared.'

'I wasn't talking about dogs, Ollie,' said the woman. 'I was talking about . . . Oh, never mind.'

'What are you drinking?' asked the landlord.

There was a handwritten piece of paper taped to the wall by the bar telling customers not to order a lager 'as a punch in the face often offends'.

'What's good and local?' asked Shadow, who had learned that this was mostly the wisest thing to say.

The landlord and the woman had various suggestions as to which of the various local beers and ciders were good. The little muttonchopped man interrupted them to point out that in his opinion *good* was not the avoidance of evil, but something more positive than that: it was making the world a better place. Then he chuckled, to show that he was only joking and that he knew that the conversation was really only about what to drink.

The beer the landlord poured for Shadow was dark and very bitter. He was not certain that he liked it. 'What is it?'

'It's called Black Dog,' said the woman. 'I've heard people say it was named after the way you feel after you've had one too many.'

'Like Churchill's moods,' said the little man.

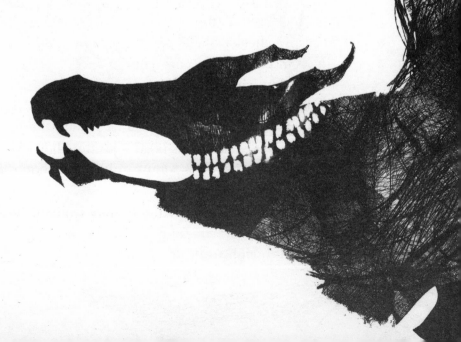

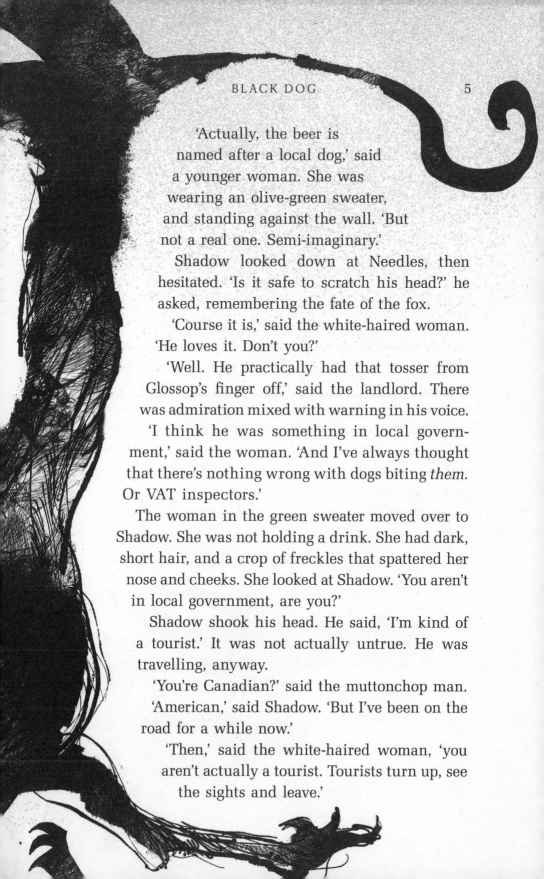

'Actually, the beer is named after a local dog,' said a younger woman. She was wearing an olive-green sweater, and standing against the wall. 'But not a real one. Semi-imaginary.'

Shadow looked down at Needles, then hesitated. 'Is it safe to scratch his head?' he asked, remembering the fate of the fox.

'Course it is,' said the white-haired woman. 'He loves it. Don't you?'

'Well. He practically had that tosser from Glossop's finger off,' said the landlord. There was admiration mixed with warning in his voice.

'I think he was something in local government,' said the woman. 'And I've always thought that there's nothing wrong with dogs biting *them*. Or VAT inspectors.'

The woman in the green sweater moved over to Shadow. She was not holding a drink. She had dark, short hair, and a crop of freckles that spattered her nose and cheeks. She looked at Shadow. 'You aren't in local government, are you?'

Shadow shook his head. He said, 'I'm kind of a tourist.' It was not actually untrue. He was travelling, anyway.

'You're Canadian?' said the muttonchop man.

'American,' said Shadow. 'But I've been on the road for a while now.'

'Then,' said the white-haired woman, 'you aren't actually a tourist. Tourists turn up, see the sights and leave.'

Shadow shrugged, smiled, and leaned down. He scratched the landlord's lurcher on the back of its head.

'You're not a dog person, are you?' asked the dark-haired woman.

'I'm not a dog person,' said Shadow.

Had he been someone else, someone who talked about what was happening inside his head, Shadow might have told her that his wife had owned dogs when she was younger, and sometimes called Shadow *puppy* because she wanted a dog she could not have. But Shadow kept things on the inside. It was one of the things he liked about the British: even when they wanted to know what was happening on the inside, they did not ask. The world on the inside remained the world on the inside. His wife had been dead for three years now.

'If you ask me,' said the man with the muttonchops, 'people are either dog people or cat people. So would you then consider yourself a cat person?'

Shadow reflected. 'I don't know. We never had pets when I was a kid, we were always on the move. But—'

'I mention this,' the man continued, 'because our host also has a cat, which you might wish to see.'

'Used to be out here, but we moved it to the back room,' said the landlord, from behind the bar.

Shadow wondered how the man could follow the conversation so easily while also taking people's meal orders and serving their drinks. 'Did the cat upset the dogs?' he asked.

Outside, the rain redoubled. The wind moaned, and whistled, and then howled. The log fire burning in the little fireplace coughed and spat.

'Not in the way you're thinking,' said the landlord. 'We found it when we knocked through into the room next door, when we needed to extend the bar.' The man grinned. 'Come and look.'

Shadow followed the man into the room next door. The muttonchop man and the white-haired woman came with them, walking a little behind Shadow.

Shadow glanced back into the bar. The dark-haired woman was watching him, and she smiled warmly when he caught her eye.

The room next door was better lit, larger, and it felt a little less like somebody's front room. People were sitting at tables, eating. The food looked good and smelled better. The landlord led Shadow to the back of the room, to a dusty glass case.

'There she is,' said the landlord, proudly.

The cat was brown, and it looked, at first glance, as if it had been constructed out of tendons and agony. The holes that were its eyes were filled with anger and with pain; the mouth was wide open, as if the creature had been yowling when she was turned to leather.

'The practice of placing animals in the walls of buildings is similar to the practice of walling up children alive in the foundations of a house you want to stay up,' explained the muttonchop man, from behind him. 'Although mummified cats always make me think of the mummified cats they found around the temple of Bast in Bubastis in Egypt. So many tons of mummified cats that they sent them to England to be ground up as cheap fertiliser and dumped on the fields. The Victorians also made paint out of mummies. A sort of brown, I believe.'

'It looks miserable,' said Shadow. 'How old is it?'

The landlord scratched his cheek. 'We reckon that the wall she was in went up somewhere between 1300 and 1600. That's from parish records. There's nothing here in 1300, and there's a house in 1600. The stuff in the middle was lost.'

The dead cat in the glass case, furless and leathery, seemed to be watching them, from its empty black-hole eyes.

I got eyes wherever my folk walk, breathed a voice in the back of Shadow's mind. He thought, momentarily, about the fields fertilised with the ground mummies of cats, and what strange crops they must have grown.

'*They put him into an old house side,*' said the man called Ollie. '*And there he lived and there he died. And nobody either laughed or cried.* All sorts of things were walled up, to make sure that things were guarded and safe. Children, sometimes. Animals. They did it in churches as a matter of course.'

The rain beat an arrhythmic rattle on the windowpane. Shadow thanked the landlord for showing him the cat. They went back into the taproom. The dark-haired woman had gone, which gave Shadow a moment of regret. She had looked so friendly. Shadow bought a round of drinks for the muttonchop man, the white-haired woman, and one for the landlord.

The landlord ducked behind the bar. 'They call me Shadow,' Shadow told them. 'Shadow Moon.'

The muttonchop man pressed his hands together in delight. 'Oh! How wonderful. I had an Alsatian named Shadow, when I was a boy. Is it your real name?'

'It's what they call me,' said Shadow.

'I'm Moira Callanish,' said the white-haired woman. 'This is my partner, Oliver Bierce. He knows a lot, and he will, during the course of our acquaintance, undoubtedly tell you everything he knows.'

They shook hands. When the landlord returned with their drinks, Shadow asked if the pub had a room to rent. He had intended to walk further that night, but the rain sounded like it had no intention of giving up. He had stout walking shoes, and weather-resistant outer clothes, but he did not want to walk in the rain.

'I used to, but then my son moved back in. I'll encourage people to sleep it off in the barn, on occasion, but that's as far as I'll go these days.'

'Anywhere in the village I could get a room?'

The landlord shook his head. 'It's a foul night. But Porsett is only a few miles down the road, and they've got a proper hotel there. I can call Sandra, tell her that you're coming. What's your name?'

'Shadow,' said Shadow again. 'Shadow Moon.'

Moira looked at Oliver, and said something that sounded like 'waifs and strays?' and Oliver chewed his lip for a moment, and then he nodded enthusiastically. 'Would you fancy spending the night with us? The spare room's a bit of a box room, but it does have a bed in it. And it's warm there. And dry.'

'I'd like that very much,' said Shadow. 'I can pay.'

'Don't be silly,' said Moira. 'It will be nice to have a guest.'

II
THE GIBBET

Oliver and Moira both had umbrellas. Oliver insisted that Shadow carry his umbrella, pointing out that Shadow towered over him, and thus was ideally suited to keep the rain off both of them.

The couple also carried little flashlights, which they called torches. The word put Shadow in mind of villagers in a horror movie storming the castle on the hill, and the lightning and thunder added to the vision. *Tonight, my creature*, he thought, *I will give you life!* It should have been hokey but instead it was disturbing. The dead cat had put him into a strange set of mind.

The narrow roads between fields were running with rainwater.

'On a nice night,' said Moira, raising her voice to be heard over the rain, 'we would just walk over the fields. But they'll be all soggy and boggy, so we're going down by Shuck's Lane. Now, that tree was a gibbet tree, once upon a time.' She pointed to a massive-trunked sycamore at the crossroads. It had only a few branches left, sticking up into the night like afterthoughts.

'Moira's lived here since she was in her twenties,' said Oliver. 'I came up from London, about eight years ago. From Turnham Green. I'd come up here on holiday originally when I was fourteen and I never forgot it. You don't.'

'The land gets into your blood,' said Moira. 'Sort of.'

'And the blood gets into the land,' said Oliver. 'One way or another. You take that gibbet tree, for example. They would leave people in the gibbet until there was nothing left. Hair gone to make bird's nests, flesh all eaten by ravens, bones picked clean. Or until they had another corpse to display anyway.'

Shadow was fairly sure he knew what a gibbet was, but he asked anyway. There was never any harm in asking, and Oliver was definitely the kind of person who took pleasure in knowing peculiar things and in passing his knowledge on.

'Like a huge iron birdcage. They used them to display the bodies of executed criminals, after justice had been served. The gibbets were locked, so the family and friends couldn't steal the body back and give it a good Christian burial. Keeping passersby on the straight and the narrow, although I doubt it actually deterred anyone from anything.'

'Who were they executing?'

'Anyone who got unlucky. Three hundred years ago, there were over two hundred crimes punishable by death. Including travelling with

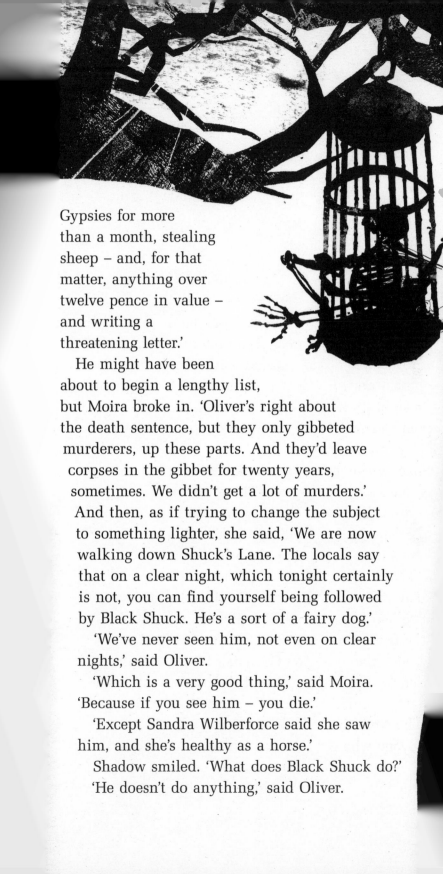

Gypsies for more than a month, stealing sheep – and, for that matter, anything over twelve pence in value – and writing a threatening letter.'

He might have been about to begin a lengthy list, but Moira broke in. 'Oliver's right about the death sentence, but they only gibbeted murderers, up these parts. And they'd leave corpses in the gibbet for twenty years, sometimes. We didn't get a lot of murders.' And then, as if trying to change the subject to something lighter, she said, 'We are now walking down Shuck's Lane. The locals say that on a clear night, which tonight certainly is not, you can find yourself being followed by Black Shuck. He's a sort of a fairy dog.'

'We've never seen him, not even on clear nights,' said Oliver.

'Which is a very good thing,' said Moira. 'Because if you see him – you die.'

'Except Sandra Wilberforce said she saw him, and she's healthy as a horse.'

Shadow smiled. 'What does Black Shuck do?'

'He doesn't do anything,' said Oliver.

'He does. He follows you home,' corrected Moira. 'And then, a bit later, you die.'

'Doesn't sound very scary,' said Shadow. 'Except for the dying bit.'

They reached the bottom of the road. Rainwater was running like a stream over Shadow's thick hiking boots.

Shadow said, 'So how did you two meet?' It was normally a safe question, when you were with couples.

Oliver said, 'In the pub. I was up here on holiday, really.'

Moira said, 'I was with someone when I met Oliver. We had a very brief, torrid affair, then we ran off together. Most unlike both of us.'

They did not seem like the kind of people who ran off together, thought Shadow. But then, all people were strange. He knew he should say something.

'I was married. My wife was killed in a car crash.'

'I'm so sorry,' said Moira.

'It happened,' said Shadow.

'When we get home,' said Moira, 'I'm making us all whisky macs. That's whisky and ginger wine and hot water. And I'm having a hot bath. Otherwise I'll catch my death.'

Shadow imagined reaching out his hand and catching death in it, like a baseball, and he shivered.

The rain redoubled, and a sudden flash of lightning burned the world into existence all around them: every grey rock in the drystone wall, every blade of grass, every puddle and every tree was perfectly illuminated, and then swallowed by a deeper darkness, leaving afterimages on Shadow's night-blinded eyes.

'Did you see that?' asked Oliver. 'Damnedest thing.' The thunder rolled and rumbled, and Shadow waited until it was done before he tried to speak.

'I didn't see anything,' said Shadow. Another flash, less bright, and Shadow thought he saw something moving away from them in a distant field. 'That?' he asked.

'It's a donkey,' said Moira. 'Only a donkey.'

Oliver stopped. He said, 'This was the wrong way to come home. We should have got a taxi. This was a mistake.'

'Ollie,' said Moira. 'It's not far now. And it's just a spot of rain. You aren't made of sugar, darling.'

Another flash of lightning, so bright as to be almost blinding. There was nothing to be seen in the fields. Darkness. Shadow turned back to Oliver, but the little man was no longer standing beside him. Oliver's flashlight was on the ground. Shadow blinked his eyes, hoping to force his night vision to return. The man had collapsed, crumpled onto the wet grass on the side of the lane.

'Ollie?' Moira crouched beside him, her umbrella by her side. She shone her flashlight onto his face. Then she looked at Shadow. 'He can't just sit here,' she said, sounding confused and concerned. 'It's pouring.'

Shadow pocketed Oliver's flashlight, handed his umbrella to Moira, then picked Oliver up. The man did not seem to weigh much, and Shadow was a big man.

'Is it far?'

'Not far,' she said. 'Not really. We're almost home.'

They walked in silence, across a churchyard on the edge of a village green, and into a village. Shadow could see lights on in the grey stone houses that edged the one street. Moira turned off, into a house set back from the road, and Shadow followed her. She held the back door open for him.

The kitchen was large and warm, and there was a sofa, half-covered with magazines, against one wall. There were low beams in the kitchen, and Shadow needed to duck his head. Shadow removed Oliver's raincoat and dropped it. It puddled on the wooden floor. Then he put the man down on the sofa.

Moira filled the kettle.

'Do we call an ambulance?'

She shook her head.

'This is just something that happens? He falls down and passes out?'

Moira busied herself getting mugs from a shelf. 'It's happened before. Just not for a long time. He's narcoleptic, and if something surprises or scares him he can just go down like that. He'll come round soon. He'll want tea. No whisky mac tonight, not for him. Sometimes he's a bit dazed and doesn't know where he is, sometimes he's been following everything that happened while he was out. And he hates it if you make a fuss. Put your backpack down by the Aga.'

The kettle boiled. Moira poured the steaming water into a teapot. 'He'll have a cup of real tea. I'll have camomile,

I think, or I won't sleep tonight. Calm my nerves. You?'

'I'll drink tea, sure,' said Shadow. He had walked more than twenty miles that day, and sleep would be easy in the finding. He wondered at Moira. She appeared perfectly self-possessed in the face of her partner's incapacity, and he wondered how much of it was not wanting to show weakness in front of a stranger. He admired her, although he found it peculiar. The English were strange. But he understood hating 'making a fuss'. Yes.

Oliver stirred on the couch. Moira was at his side with a cup of tea, helped him into a sitting position. He sipped the tea, in a slightly dazed fashion.

'It followed me home,' he said, conversationally.

'What followed you, Ollie, darling?' Her voice was steady, but there was concern in it.

'The dog,' said the man on the sofa, and he took another sip of his tea. 'The black dog.'

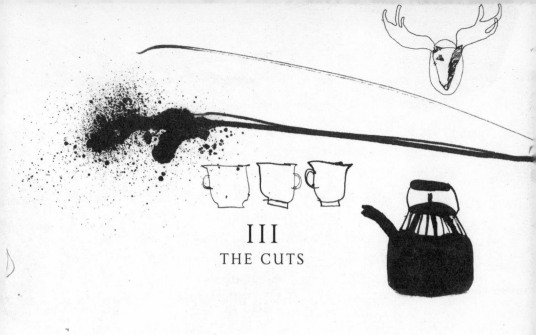

III
THE CUTS

These were the things Shadow learned that night, sitting around the kitchen table with Moira and Oliver:

He learned that Oliver had not been happy or fulfilled in his London advertising agency job. He had moved up to the village and taken an extremely early medical retirement. Now, initially for recreation and increasingly for money, he repaired and rebuilt drystone walls. There was, he explained, an art and a skill to wall building, it was excellent exercise, and, when done correctly, a meditative practice.

'There used to be hundreds of drystone-wall people around here. Now there's barely a dozen who know what they're doing. You see walls repaired with concrete, or with breeze blocks. It's a dying art. I'd love to show you how I do it. Useful skill to have. Picking the rock, sometimes, you have to let the rock tell you where it goes. And then it's immovable. You couldn't knock it down with a tank. Remarkable.'

He learned that Oliver had been very depressed several

years earlier, shortly after Moira and he got together, but that for the last few years he had been doing very well. Or, he amended, relatively well.

He learned that Moira was independently wealthy, that her family trust fund had meant that she and her sisters had not needed to work, but that, in her late twenties, she had gone for teacher training. That she no longer taught, but that she was extremely active in local affairs, and had campaigned successfully to keep the local bus routes in service.

Shadow learned, from what Oliver didn't say, that Oliver was scared of something, very scared, and that when Oliver was asked what had frightened him so badly, and what he had meant by saying that the black dog had followed him home, his response was to stammer and to sway. He learned not to ask Oliver any more questions.

This is what Oliver and Moira had learned about Shadow sitting around that kitchen table:

Nothing much.

Shadow liked them. He was not a stupid man; he had trusted people in the past who had betrayed him but he liked this couple, and he liked the way their home smelled – like bread-making and jam and walnut wood-polish – and he went to sleep that night in his box-room bedroom worrying about the little man with the muttonchop beard. What if the thing Shadow had glimpsed in the field had *not* been a donkey? What if it *had* been an enormous dog? What then?

The rain had stopped when Shadow woke. He made himself toast in the empty kitchen. Moira came in from the garden, letting a gust of chilly air in through the kitchen door. 'Sleep well?' she asked.

'Yes. Very well.' He had dreamed of being at the zoo. He had been surrounded by animals he could not see, which snuffled and snorted in their pens. He was a child, walking with his mother, and he was safe and he was loved. He had stopped in front of a lion's cage, but what had been in the cage was a sphinx, half lion and half woman, her tail swishing. She had smiled at him, and her smile had been his mother's smile. He heard her voice, accented and warm and feline.

It said, *Know thyself.*

I know who I am, said Shadow in his dream, holding the bars of the cage. Behind the bars was the desert. He could see pyramids. He could see shadows on the sand.

Then who are you, Shadow? What are you running from? Where are you running to?

Who are you?

And he had woken, wondering why he was asking himself that question, and missing his mother, who had died twenty years before, when he was a teenager. He still felt oddly comforted, remembering the feel of his hand in his mother's hand.

'I'm afraid Ollie's a bit under the weather this morning.'

'Sorry to hear that.'

'Yes. Well, can't be helped.'

'I'm really grateful for the room. I guess I'll be on my way.'

Moira said, 'Will you look at something for me?'

Shadow nodded, then followed her outside, and round the side of the house. She pointed to the rose bed. 'What does that look like to you?'

Shadow bent down. *'The footprint of an enormous hound,'* he said. 'To quote Dr Watson.'

'Yes,' she said. 'It really does.'

'If there's a spectral ghost-hound out there,' said Shadow, 'it shouldn't leave footprints. Should it?'

'I'm not actually an authority on these matters,' said Moira. 'I had a friend once who could have told us all about it. But she . . .' She trailed off. Then, more brightly, 'You know, Mrs Camberley two doors down has a Doberman pinscher. Ridiculous thing.' Shadow was not certain whether the ridiculous thing was Mrs Camberley or her dog.

He found the events of the previous night less troubling

and odd, more explicable. What did it matter if a strange dog had followed them home? Oliver had been frightened or startled, and had collapsed, from narcolepsy, from shock.

'Well, I'll pack you some lunch before you go,' said Moira. 'Boiled eggs. That sort of thing. You'll be glad of them on the way.'

They went into the house. Moira went to put something away, and returned looking shaken.

'Oliver's locked himself in the bathroom,' she said.

Shadow was not certain what to say.

'You know what I wish?' she continued.

'I don't.'

'I wish you would talk to him. I wish he would open the door. I wish he'd talk to me. I can hear him in there. I can hear him.'

And then, 'I hope he isn't cutting himself again.'

Shadow walked back into the hall, stood by the bathroom door, called Oliver's name. 'Can you hear me? Are you okay?'

Nothing. No sound from inside.

Shadow looked at the door. It was solid wood. The house was old, and they built them strong and well back then. When Shadow had used the bathroom that morning he'd learned the lock was a hook and eye. He leaned on the handle of the door, pushing it down, then rammed his shoulder against the door. It opened with a noise of splintering wood.

He had watched a man die in prison, stabbed in a pointless argument. He remembered the way that the blood had puddled about the man's body, lying in the back corner of the exercise yard. The sight had troubled Shadow, but he had forced himself to look, and to keep looking. To look away would somehow have felt disrespectful.

Oliver was naked on the floor of the bathroom. His body was pale, and his chest and groin were covered with thick, dark hair. He held the blade from an ancient safety razor in his hands. He had sliced his arms with it, his chest above the nipples, his inner thighs and his penis. Blood was smeared on his body, on the black-and-white linoleum floor, on the white enamel of the bathtub. Oliver's eyes were round and wide, like the eyes of a bird. He was looking directly at Shadow, but Shadow was not certain that he was being seen.

'Ollie?' said Moira's voice, from the hall. Shadow realised that he was blocking the doorway and he hesitated, unsure whether to let her see what was on the floor or not.

Shadow took a pink towel from the towel rail and wrapped it around Oliver. That got the little man's attention. He blinked, as if seeing Shadow for the first time, and said, 'The dog. It's for the dog. It must be fed, you see. We're making friends.'

Moira said, 'Oh my dear sweet god.'

'I'll call the emergency services.'

'Please don't,' she said. 'He'll be fine at home with me. I don't know what I'll . . . please?'

Shadow picked up Oliver, swaddled in the towel, carried him into the bedroom as if he were a child, and then placed him on the bed. Moira followed. She picked up an iPad by the bed, touched the screen, and music began to play. 'Breathe, Ollie,' she said. 'Remember. Breathe. It's going to be fine. You're going to be fine.'

'I can't really breathe,' said Oliver, in a small voice. 'Not really. I can feel my heart, though. I can feel my heart beating.'

Moira squeezed his hand and sat down on the bed, and Shadow left them alone.

When Moira entered the kitchen, her sleeves rolled up, and her hands smelling of antiseptic cream, Shadow was sitting on the sofa, reading a guide to local walks.

'How's he doing?'

She shrugged.

'You have to get him help.'

'Yes.' She stood in the middle of the kitchen and looked about her, as if unable to decide which way to turn. 'Do you . . . I mean, do you have to leave today? Are you on a schedule?'

'Nobody's waiting for me. Anywhere.'

She looked at him with a face that had grown haggard

in an hour. 'When this happened before, it took a few days, but then he was right as rain. The depression doesn't stay long. So, just wondering, would you just, well, stick around? I phoned my sister but she's in the middle of moving. And I can't cope on my own. I really can't. Not again. But I can't ask you to stay, not if anyone is waiting for you.'

'Nobody's waiting,' repeated Shadow. 'And I'll stick around. But I think Oliver needs specialist help.'

'Yes,' agreed Moira. 'He does.'

Dr Scathelocke came over late that afternoon. He was a friend of Oliver and Moira's. Shadow was not entirely certain whether rural British doctors still made house calls, or whether this was a socially justified visit. The doctor went into the bedroom, and came out twenty minutes later.

He sat at the kitchen table with Moira, and he said, 'It's all very shallow. Cry-for-help stuff. Honestly, there's not a lot we can do for him in hospital that you can't do for him here, what with the cuts. We used to have a dozen nurses in that wing. Now they are trying to close it down completely. Get it all back to the community.' Dr Scathelocke had sandy hair, was as tall as Shadow but lankier. He reminded Shadow of the landlord in the pub, and he wondered idly if the two men were related. The doctor scribbled several prescriptions, and Moira handed them to Shadow, along with the keys to an old white Range Rover.

Shadow drove to the next village, found the little chemists' and waited for the prescriptions to be filled. He stood awkwardly in the overlit aisle, staring at a display of suntan lotions and creams, sadly redundant in this cold wet summer.

'You're Mr American,' said a woman's voice from behind him. He turned. She had short dark hair and was wearing the same olive-green sweater she had been wearing in the pub.

'I guess I am,' he said.

'Local gossip says that you are helping out while Ollie's under the weather.'

'That was fast.'

'Local gossip travels faster than light. I'm Cassie Burglass.'

'Shadow Moon.'

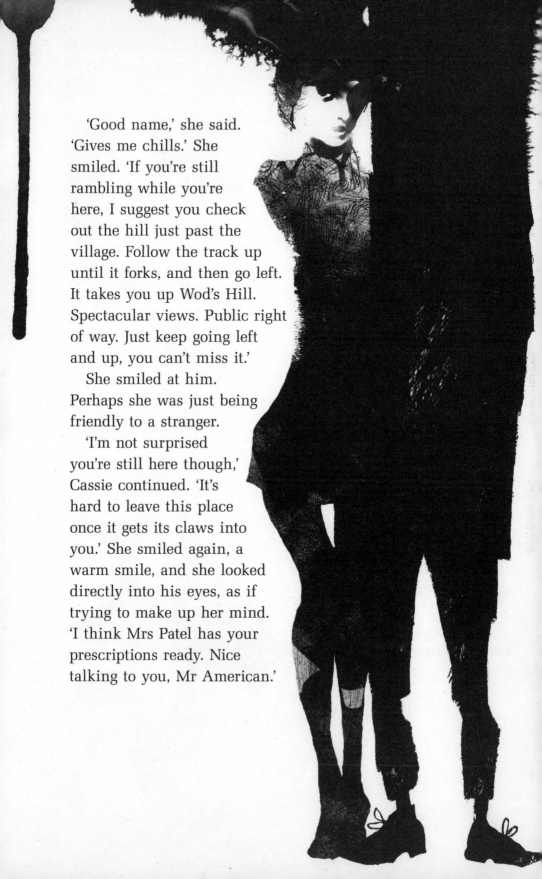

'Good name,' she said. 'Gives me chills.' She smiled. 'If you're still rambling while you're here, I suggest you check out the hill just past the village. Follow the track up until it forks, and then go left. It takes you up Wod's Hill. Spectacular views. Public right of way. Just keep going left and up, you can't miss it.'

She smiled at him. Perhaps she was just being friendly to a stranger.

'I'm not surprised you're still here though,' Cassie continued. 'It's hard to leave this place once it gets its claws into you.' She smiled again, a warm smile, and she looked directly into his eyes, as if trying to make up her mind. 'I think Mrs Patel has your prescriptions ready. Nice talking to you, Mr American.'

IV
THE KISS

Shadow helped Moira. He walked down to the village shop and bought the items on her shopping list while she stayed in the house, writing at the kitchen table or hovering in the hallway outside the bedroom door. Moira barely talked. He ran errands in the white Range Rover, and saw Oliver mostly in the hall, shuffling to the bathroom and back. The man did not speak to him.

Everything was quiet in the house: Shadow imagined the black dog squatting on the roof, cutting out all sunlight, all emotion, all feeling and truth. Something had turned down the volume in that house, pushed all the colours into black and white. He wished he was somewhere else, but could not run out on them. He sat on his bed, and stared out of the window at the rain puddling its way down the windowpane, and felt the seconds of his life counting off, never to come back.

It had been wet and cold, but on the third day the sun came out. The world did not warm up, but Shadow tried to pull himself out of the grey haze, and

decided to see some of the local sights. He walked to the
next village, through fields, up paths and along the side of
a long drystone wall. There was a bridge over a narrow
stream that was little more than a plank, and Shadow
jumped the water in one easy bound. Up the hill: there
were trees, oak and hawthorn, sycamore and beech at the
bottom of the hill, and then the trees became sparser. He
followed the winding trail, sometimes obvious, sometimes
not, until he reached a natural resting place, like a tiny
meadow, high on the hill, and there he turned away from
the hill and saw the valleys and the peaks arranged all
about him in greens and greys like illustrations from a
children's book.

He was not alone up there. A woman with short dark
hair was sitting and sketching on the hill's side, perched
comfortably on a grey boulder. There was a tree behind
her, which acted as a windbreak. She wore a green sweater
and blue jeans, and he recognised Cassie Burglass before
he saw her face.

As he got close, she turned. 'What do you think?' she
asked, holding her sketchbook up for his inspection. It
was an assured pencil drawing of the hillside.

'You're very good. Are you a professional artist?'

'I dabble,' she said.

Shadow had spent enough time talking to the English
to know that this meant either that she dabbled, or that
her work was regularly hung in the National Gallery or
Tate Modern.

'You must be cold,' he said. 'You're only wearing a sweater.'

'I'm cold,' she said. 'But, up here, I'm used to it. It doesn't
really bother me. How's Ollie doing?'

'He's still under the weather,' Shadow told her.

'Poor old sod,' she said, looking from her paper to the hillside and back. 'It's hard for me to feel properly sorry for him, though.'

'Why's that? Did he bore you to death with interesting facts?'

She laughed, a small huff of air at the back of her throat. 'You really ought to listen to more village gossip. When Ollie and Moira met, they were both with other people.'

'I know that. They told me that.' Shadow thought a moment. 'So he was with you first?'

'No. *She* was. We'd been together since college.' There was a pause. She shaded something, her pencil scraping the paper. 'Are you going to try and kiss me?' she asked.

'I, uh. I, um,' he said. Then, honestly, 'It hadn't occurred to me.'

'Well,' she said, turning to smile at him, 'it bloody well should. I mean, I asked you up here, and you came, up to Wod's Hill, just to see me.' She went back to the paper and the drawing of the hill. 'They say there's dark doings been done on this hill. Dirty dark doings. And I was thinking of doing something dirty myself. To Moira's lodger.'

'Is this some kind of revenge plot?'

'It's not an anything plot. I just like you. And there's no one around here who wants me any longer. Not as a woman.'

The last woman that Shadow had kissed had been in Scotland. He thought of her, and what she had become, in the end. 'You *are* real, aren't you?' he asked. 'I mean . . . you're a real person. I mean . . .'

She put the pad of paper down on the boulder and she stood up. 'Kiss me and find out,' she said.

He hesitated. She sighed, and she kissed him.

It was cold on that hillside, and Cassie's lips were cold. Her mouth was very soft. As her tongue touched his, Shadow pulled back.

'I don't actually know you,' Shadow said.

She leaned away from him, looked up into his face. 'You know,' she said, 'all I dream of these days is somebody who will look my way and see the real me. I had given up until you came along, Mr American, with your funny name. But you looked at me, and I knew you saw me. And that's all that matters.'

Shadow's hands held her, feeling the softness of her sweater.

'How much longer are you going to be here? In the district?' she asked.

'A few more days. Until Oliver's feeling better.'

'Pity. Can't you stay forever?'

'I'm sorry?'

'You have nothing to be sorry for, sweet man. You see that opening over there?'

He glanced over to the hillside, but could not see what she was pointing at. The hillside was a tangle of weeds and low trees and half-tumbled drystone walls. She pointed to her drawing, where she had drawn a dark shape, like an archway, in the middle of a clump of gorse bushes on the side of the hill. 'There. Look.' He stared, and this time he saw it immediately.

'What is it?' Shadow asked.

'The Gateway to Hell,' she told him, impressively.

'Uh-huh.'

She grinned. 'That's what they call it round here. It was originally a Roman temple, I think, or something even older. But that's all that remains. You should check it out,

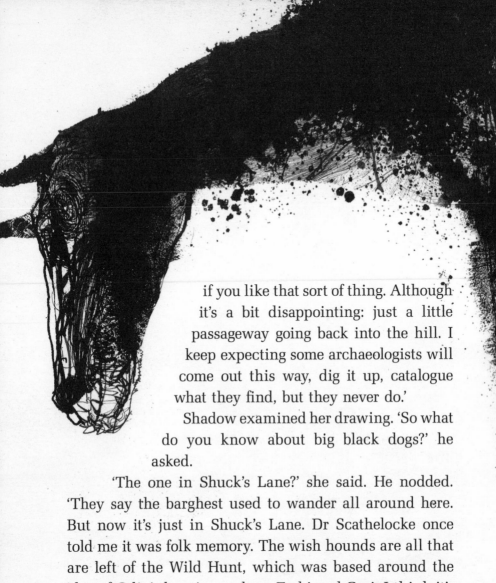

if you like that sort of thing. Although it's a bit disappointing: just a little passageway going back into the hill. I keep expecting some archaeologists will come out this way, dig it up, catalogue what they find, but they never do.'

Shadow examined her drawing. 'So what do you know about big black dogs?' he asked.

'The one in Shuck's Lane?' she said. He nodded. 'They say the barghest used to wander all around here. But now it's just in Shuck's Lane. Dr Scathelocke once told me it was folk memory. The wish hounds are all that are left of the Wild Hunt, which was based around the idea of Odin's hunting wolves, Freki and Geri. I think it's even older than that. Cave memory. Druids. The thing that prowls in the darkness beyond the fire circle, waiting to tear you apart if you edge too far out alone.'

'Have you ever seen it, then?'

She shook her head. 'No. I researched it, but never saw it. My semi-imaginary local beast. Have you?'

'I don't think so. Maybe.'

'Perhaps you woke it up when you came here. You woke me up, after all.'

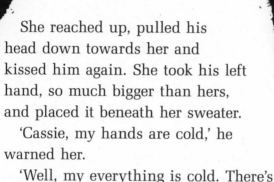

She reached up, pulled his
head down towards her and
kissed him again. She took his left
hand, so much bigger than hers,
and placed it beneath her sweater.

'Cassie, my hands are cold,' he
warned her.

'Well, my everything is cold. There's
nothing *but* cold up here. Just smile and
look like you know what you're doing,' she
told him. She pushed Shadow's left hand
higher, until it was cupping the lace of her bra,
and he could feel, beneath the lace, the hardness of
her nipple and the soft swell of her breast.

He began to surrender to the moment, his hesitation a
mixture of awkwardness and uncertainty. He was not sure
how he felt about this woman: she had history with his
benefactors, after all. Shadow never liked feeling that he
was being used; it had happened too many times before.
But his left hand was touching her breast and his right
hand was cradling the nape of her neck, and he was
leaning down and now her mouth was on his, and she
was clinging to him as tightly as if, he thought, she wanted
to occupy the very same space that he was in. Her mouth

tasted like mint and stone and grass and the chilly afternoon breeze. He closed his eyes, and let himself enjoy the kiss and the way their bodies moved together.

Cassie froze. Somewhere close to them, a cat mewed. Shadow opened his eyes.

'Jesus,' he said.

They were surrounded by cats. White cats and tabbies, brown and ginger and black cats, long haired and short. Well-fed cats with collars and disreputable ragged-eared cats that looked as if they had been living in barns and on the edges of the wild. They stared at Shadow and Cassie with green eyes and blue eyes and golden eyes, and they did not move. Only the occasional swish of a tail or the blinking of a pair of feline eyes told Shadow that they were alive.

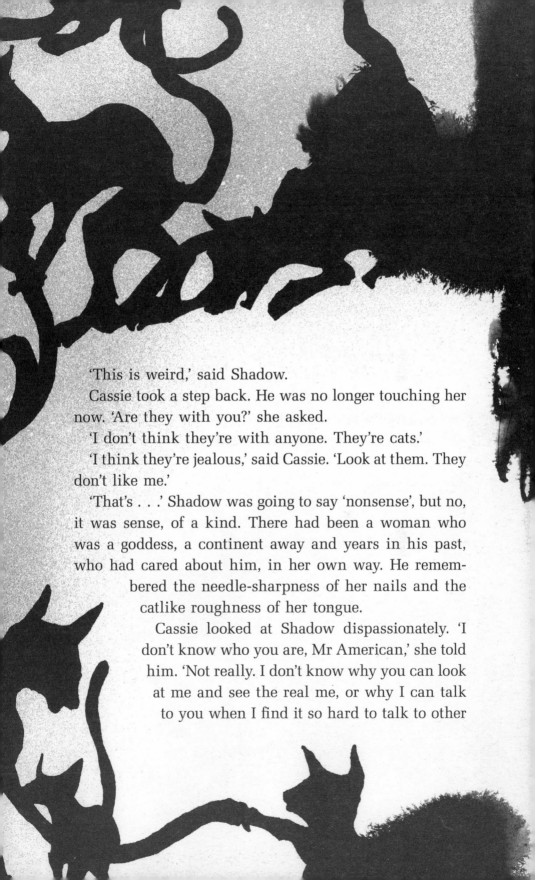

'This is weird,' said Shadow.

Cassie took a step back. He was no longer touching her now. 'Are they with you?' she asked.

'I don't think they're with anyone. They're cats.'

'I think they're jealous,' said Cassie. 'Look at them. They don't like me.'

'That's . . .' Shadow was going to say 'nonsense', but no, it was sense, of a kind. There had been a woman who was a goddess, a continent away and years in his past, who had cared about him, in her own way. He remembered the needle-sharpness of her nails and the catlike roughness of her tongue.

Cassie looked at Shadow dispassionately. 'I don't know who you are, Mr American,' she told him. 'Not really. I don't know why you can look at me and see the real me, or why I can talk to you when I find it so hard to talk to other people. But I can. And you know, you seem all normal and quiet on the surface, but you are so much weirder than I am. And I'm extremely fucking weird.'

Shadow said, 'Don't go.'

'Tell Ollie and Moira you saw me,' she said. 'Tell them I'll be waiting where we last spoke, if they have anything they want to say to me.' She picked up her sketchpad and pencils, and she walked off briskly, stepping carefully through the cats, who did not even glance at her, just kept their gazes fixed on Shadow, as she moved away through the swaying grasses and the blowing twigs.

Shadow wanted to call after her, but instead he crouched down and looked back at the cats. 'What's going on?' he asked. 'Bast? Are you doing this? You're a long way from home. And why would you still care who I kiss?'

The spell was broken when he spoke. The cats began to move, to look away, to stand, to wash themselves intently.

A tortoiseshell cat pushed her head against his hand, insistently, needing attention. Shadow stroked her absently, rubbing his knuckles against her forehead.

She swiped blinding-fast with claws like tiny scimitars, and drew blood from his forearm. Then she purred, and turned, and within moments the whole kit and caboodle of them had vanished into the hillside, slipping behind rocks and into the undergrowth, and were gone.

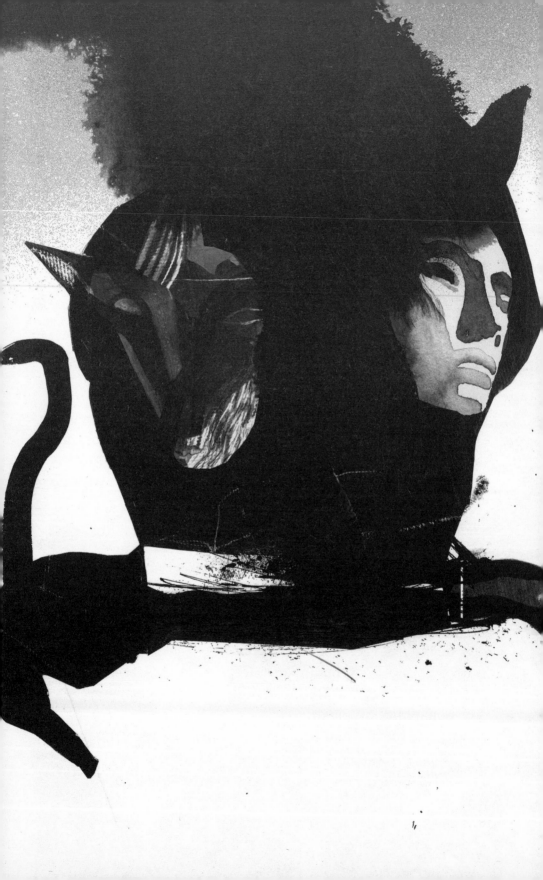

V

THE LIVING AND THE DEAD

Oliver was out of his room when Shadow got back to the house, sitting in the warm kitchen, a mug of tea by his side, reading a book on Roman architecture. He was dressed, and he had shaved his chin and trimmed his beard. He was wearing pyjamas, with a plaid bathrobe over them.

'I'm feeling a bit better,' he said, when he saw Shadow. Then, 'Have you ever had this? Been depressed?'

'Looking back on it, I guess I did. When my wife died,' said Shadow. 'Everything went flat. Nothing meant anything for a long time.'

Oliver nodded. 'It's hard. Sometimes I think the black dog is a real thing. I lie in bed thinking about the painting of Fuseli's nightmare on a sleeper's chest. Like Anubis. Or do I mean Set? Big black thing. What was Set anyway? Some kind of donkey?'

'I never ran into Set,' said Shadow. 'He was before my time.'

Oliver laughed. 'Very dry. And they say you Americans

don't do irony.' He paused. 'Anyway. All done now. Back on my feet. Ready to face the world.' He sipped his tea. 'Feeling a bit embarrassed. All that Hound of the Baskervilles nonsense behind me now.'

'You really have nothing to be embarrassed about,' said Shadow, reflecting that the English found embarrassment wherever they looked for it.

'Well. All a bit silly, one way or another. And I really am feeling much perkier.'

Shadow nodded. 'If you're feeling better, I guess I should start heading south.'

'No hurry,' said Oliver. 'It's always nice to have company. Moira and I don't really get out as much as we'd like. It's mostly just a walk up to the pub. Not much excitement here, I'm afraid.'

Moira came in from the garden. 'Anyone seen the secateurs? I know I had them. Forget my own head next.'

Shadow shook his head, uncertain what secateurs were. He thought of telling the couple about the cats on the hill, and how they had behaved, but could not think of a way to describe it that would explain how odd it was. So, instead, without thinking, he said, 'I ran into Cassie Burglass on Wod's Hill. She pointed out the Gateway to Hell.'

They were staring at him. The kitchen had become awkwardly quiet. He said, 'She was drawing it.'

Oliver looked at him and said, 'I don't understand.'

'I've run into her a couple of times since I got here,' said Shadow.

'What?' Moira's face was flushed. 'What are you saying?' And then, 'Who the, who the *fuck* are you to come in here and say things like that?'

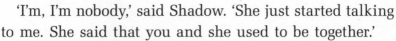

'I'm, I'm nobody,' said Shadow. 'She just started talking to me. She said that you and she used to be together.'

Moira looked as if she were going to hit him. Then she just said, 'She moved away after we broke up. It wasn't a good breakup. She was very hurt. She behaved appallingly. Then she just up and left the village in the night. Never came back.'

'I don't want to talk about that woman,' said Oliver, quietly. 'Not now. Not ever.'

'Look. She was in the pub with us,' pointed out Shadow. 'That first night. You guys didn't seem to have a problem with her then.'

Moira just stared at him and did not respond, as if he had said something in a tongue she did not speak. Oliver rubbed his forehead with his hand. 'I didn't see her,' was all he said.

'Well, she said to say hi when I saw her today,' said Shadow. 'She said she'd be waiting, if either of you had anything you wanted to say to her.'

'We have nothing to say to her. Nothing at all.' Moira's eyes were wet, but she was not crying. 'I can't believe that, that *fucking* woman has come back into our lives, after all she put us through.' Moira swore like someone who was not very good at it.

Oliver put down his book. 'I'm sorry,' he said. 'I don't feel very well.' He walked out, back to the bedroom, and closed the door behind him.

Moira picked up Oliver's mug, almost automatically, and took it over to the sink, emptied it out and began to wash it.

'I hope you're pleased with yourself,' she said, rubbing the mug with a white plastic scrubbing brush as if she

were trying to scrub the picture of Beatrix Potter's cottage from the china. 'He was coming back to himself again.'

'I didn't know it would upset him like that,' said Shadow. He felt guilty as he said it. He had known there was history between Cassie and his hosts. He could have said nothing, after all. Silence was always safer.

Moira dried the mug with a green and white tea towel. The white patches of the towel were comical sheep, the green were grass. She bit her lower lip, and the tears that had been brimming in her eyes now ran down her cheeks. Then, 'Did she say anything about me?'

'Just that you two used to be an item.'

Moira nodded, and wiped the tears from her young-old face with the comical tea towel. 'She couldn't bear it when Ollie and I got together. After I moved out, she just hung up her paintbrushes and locked the flat and went to

London.' She blew her nose vigorously. 'Still. Mustn't grumble. We make our own beds. And Ollie's a *good* man. There's just a black dog in his mind. My mother had depression. It's hard.'

Shadow said, 'I've made everything worse. I should go.'

'Don't leave until tomorrow. I'm not throwing you out, dear. It's not your fault you ran into that woman, is it?' Her shoulders were slumped. 'There they are. On top of the fridge.' She picked up something that looked like a very small pair of garden shears. 'Secateurs,' she explained. 'For the rosebushes, mostly.'

'Are you going to talk to him?'

'No,' she said. 'Conversations with Ollie about Cassie never end well. And in this state, it could plunge him even further back into a bad place. I'll just let him get over it.'

Shadow ate alone in the pub that night, while the cat in the glass case glowered at him. He saw no one he knew. He had a brief conversation with the landlord about how he was enjoying his time in the village. He walked back to Moira's house after the pub, past the old sycamore, the gibbet tree, down Shuck's Lane. He saw nothing moving in the fields in the moonlight: no dog, no donkey.

All the lights in the house were out. He went to his bedroom as quietly as he could, packed the last of his possessions into his backpack before he went to sleep. He would leave early, he knew.

He lay in bed, watching the moonlight in the box room. He remembered standing in the pub, and Cassie Burglass standing beside him. He thought about his conversation with the landlord, and the conversation that first night, and the cat in the glass box, and, as he pondered, any desire to sleep evaporated. He was perfectly wide awake in the small bed.

Shadow could move quietly when he needed to. He slipped out of bed, pulled on his clothes and then, carrying his boots, he opened the window, reached over the sill and let himself tumble silently into the soil of the flower bed beneath. He got to his feet and put on the boots, lacing them up in the half dark. The moon was several days from full, bright enough to cast shadows.

Shadow stepped into a patch of darkness beside a wall, and he waited there.

He wondered how sane his actions were. It seemed very probable that he was wrong, that his memory had played tricks on him, or other people's had. It was all so very unlikely, but then, he had experienced the unlikely before, and if he was wrong he would be out, what? A few hours' sleep?

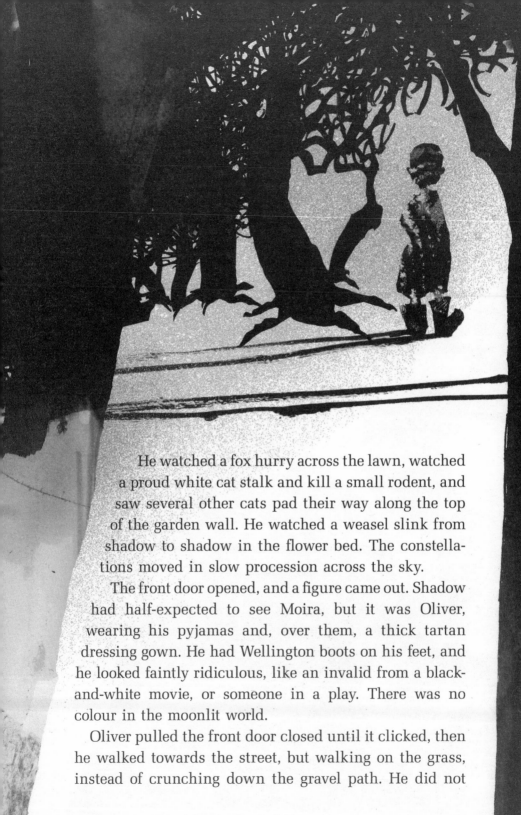

He watched a fox hurry across the lawn, watched a proud white cat stalk and kill a small rodent, and saw several other cats pad their way along the top of the garden wall. He watched a weasel slink from shadow to shadow in the flower bed. The constellations moved in slow procession across the sky.

The front door opened, and a figure came out. Shadow had half-expected to see Moira, but it was Oliver, wearing his pyjamas and, over them, a thick tartan dressing gown. He had Wellington boots on his feet, and he looked faintly ridiculous, like an invalid from a black-and-white movie, or someone in a play. There was no colour in the moonlit world.

Oliver pulled the front door closed until it clicked, then he walked towards the street, but walking on the grass, instead of crunching down the gravel path. He did not

glance back, or even look around. He set off up the lane, and Shadow waited until Oliver was almost out of sight before he began to follow. He knew where Oliver was going, had to be going.

Shadow did not question himself, not any longer. He knew where they were both headed, with the certainty of a person in a dream. He was not even surprised when, halfway up Wod's Hill, he found Oliver sitting on a tree stump, waiting for him. The sky was lightening, just a little, in the east.

'The Gateway to Hell,' said the little man. 'As far as I can tell, they've always called it that. Goes back years and years.'

The two men walked up the winding path together. There was something gloriously comical about Oliver in his robe, in his striped pyjamas and his oversized black rubber boots. Shadow's heart pumped in his chest.

'How did you bring her up here?' asked Shadow.

'Cassie? I didn't. It was her idea to meet up here on the hill. She loved coming up here to paint. You can see so far. And it's holy, this hill, and she always loved that. Not holy to Christians, of course. Quite the obverse. The old religion.'

'Druids?' asked Shadow. He was uncertain what other old religions there were, in England.

'Could be. Definitely could be. But I think it predates the druids. Doesn't have much of a name. It's just what people in these parts practise, beneath whatever else they believe. Druids, Norse, Catholics, Protestants, doesn't matter. That's what people pay lip service to. The old religion is what gets the crops up and keeps your cock hard and makes sure that nobody builds a bloody great motorway through an area of outstanding natural beauty. The Gateway stands, and the hill stands, and the place stands. It's well, well over two thousand years old. You don't go mucking about with anything that powerful.'

Shadow said, 'Moira doesn't know, does she? She thinks Cassie moved away.' The sky was continuing to lighten in the east, but it was still night, spangled with a glitter of stars, in the purple-black sky to the west.

'That was what she *needed* to think. I mean, what else was she going to think? It might have been different if the police had been interested . . . but it wasn't like . . . Well. It protects itself. The hill. The gate.'

They were coming up to the little meadow on the side of the hill. They passed the boulder where Shadow had seen Cassie drawing. They walked towards the hill.

'The black dog in Shuck's Lane,' said Oliver. 'I don't actually think it is a dog. But it's been there so long.' He pulled out a small LED flashlight from the pocket of his bathrobe. 'You really talked to Cassie?'

'We talked, I even kissed her.'

'Strange.'

'I first saw her in the pub, the night I met you and Moira. That was what made me start to figure it out. Earlier tonight, Moira was talking as if she hadn't seen Cassie in years. She was baffled when I asked. But Cassie was standing just behind me that first night, and she spoke to us. Tonight, I asked at the pub if Cassie had been in, and nobody knew who I was talking about. You people all know each other. It was the only thing that made sense of it all. It made sense of what she said. Everything.'

Oliver was almost at the place Cassie had called the Gateway to Hell. 'I thought that it would be so simple. I would give her to the hill, and she would leave us both alone. Leave Moira alone. How could she have kissed you?'

Shadow said nothing.

'This is it,' said Oliver. It was a hollow in the side of the hill, like a short hallway that went back. Perhaps, once, long ago, there had been a structure, but the hill had weathered, and the stones had returned to the hill from which they had been taken.

'There are those who think it's devil worship,' said Oliver. 'And I think they are wrong. But then, one man's god is another's devil. Eh?'

He walked into the passageway, and Shadow followed him.

'Such bullshit,' said a woman's voice. 'But you always were a bullshitter, Ollie, you pusillanimous little cock-stain.'

Oliver did not move or react. He said, 'She's here. In the wall. That's where I left her.' He shone the flashlight

at the wall, in the short passageway into the side of the hill. He inspected the drystone wall carefully, as if he were looking for a place he recognised, then he made a little grunting noise of recognition. Oliver took out a compact metal tool from his pocket, reached as high as he could and levered out one little rock with it. Then he began to pull rocks out from the wall, in a set sequence, each rock opening a space to allow another to be removed, alternating large rocks and small.

'Give me a hand. Come on.'

Shadow knew what he was going to see behind the wall, but he pulled out the rocks, placed them down on the ground, one by one.

There was a smell, which intensified as the hole grew bigger, a stink of old rot and mould. It smelled like meat sandwiches gone bad. Shadow saw her face first, and he barely knew it as a face: the cheeks were sunken, the eyes gone, the skin now dark and leathery, and if there were freckles they were impossible to make out; but the hair was Cassie Burglass's hair, short and black, and in the LED light, he could see that the dead thing wore an olive-green sweater, and the blue jeans were her blue jeans.

'It's funny. I knew she was still here,' said Oliver. 'But I still had to see her. With all your talk. I had to see it. To prove she was still here.'

'Kill him,' said the woman's voice. 'Hit him with a rock, Shadow. He killed me. Now he's going to kill you.'

'Are you going to kill me?' Shadow asked.

'Well, yes, obviously,' said the little man, in his sensible voice. 'I mean, you know about Cassie. And once you're gone, I can just finally forget about the whole thing, once and for all.'

'Forget?'

'Forgive *and* forget. But it's hard. It's not easy to forgive myself, but I'm sure I can forget. There. I think there's enough room for you to get in there now, if you squeeze.'

Shadow looked down at the little man. 'Out of interest,' he said, curious, 'how are you going to make me get in there? You don't have a gun on you. And, Ollie, I'm twice your size. You know, I could just break your neck.'

'I'm not a stupid man,' said Oliver. 'I'm not a bad man, either. I'm not a terribly well man, but that's neither here nor there, really. I mean, I did what I did because I was jealous, not because I was ill. But I wouldn't have come up here alone. You see, this is the temple of the Black Dog. These places were the first temples. Before the stone henges and the standing stones, they were waiting and they were worshipped, and sacrificed to, and feared, and placated. The black shucks and the barghests, the padfoots and the wish hounds. They were here and they remain on guard.'

'Hit him with a rock,' said Cassie's voice. 'Hit him now, Shadow, *please.*'

The passage they stood in went a little way into the hillside, a man-made cave with drystone walls. It did not look like an ancient temple. It did not look like a gateway to hell. The predawn sky framed Oliver. In his gentle, unfailingly polite voice, he said, 'He is in me. And I am in him.'

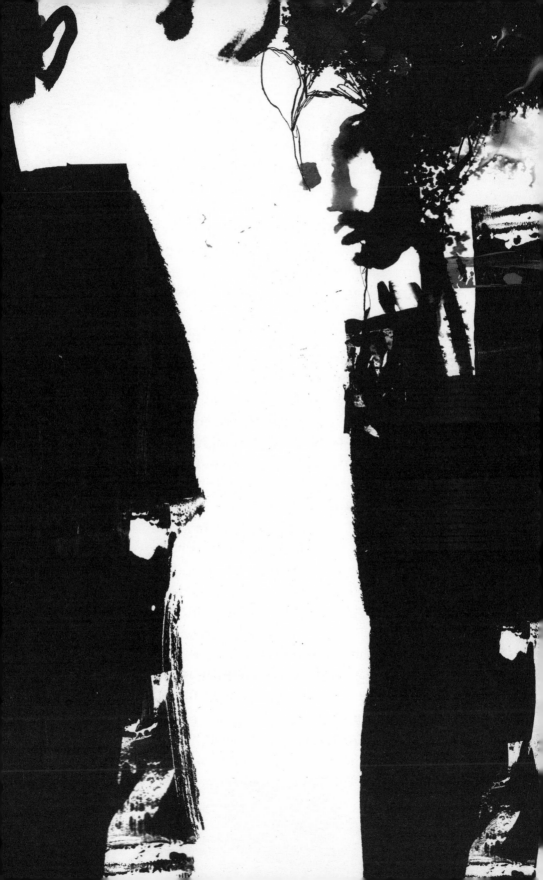

The black dog filled
the doorway, blocking the
way to the world outside, and, Shadow
knew, whatever it was, it was no true dog. Its eyes
actually glowed, with a luminescence that reminded
Shadow of rotting sea-creatures. It was to a wolf, in scale
and in menace, what a tiger is to a lynx: pure carnivore,
a creature made of danger and threat. It stood taller than
Oliver and it stared at Shadow, and it growled, a rumbling
deep in its chest. Then it sprang.

Shadow raised his arm to protect his throat, and the
creature sank its teeth into his flesh, just below the elbow.
The pain was excruciating. He knew he should fight back,
but he was falling to his knees, and he was screaming,
unable to think clearly, unable to focus on anything except
his fear that the creature was going to use him for food,
fear it was crushing the bone of his forearm.

On some deep level he suspected that the fear was being
created by the dog: that he, Shadow, was not cripplingly
afraid like that. Not really. But it did not matter. When
the creature released Shadow's arm, he was weeping and
his whole body was shaking.

Oliver said, 'Get in there, Shadow. Through the gap in
the wall. Quickly, now. Or I'll have him chew off your
face.'

Shadow's arm was bleeding, but he got up and squeezed
through the gap into the darkness without arguing. If he
stayed out there, with the beast, he would die soon, and
die in pain. He knew that with as much certainty as he
knew that the sun would rise tomorrow.

'Well, yes,' said Cassie's voice in his head. 'It's going to rise. But unless you get your shit together you are never going to see it.'

There was barely space for him and Cassie's body in the cavity behind the wall. He had seen the expression of pain and fury on her face, like the face of the cat in the glass box, and then he knew she, too, had been entombed here while alive.

Oliver picked up a rock from the ground, and placed it onto the wall, in the gap. 'My own theory,' he said, hefting a second rock and putting it into position, 'is that it is the prehistoric dire wolf. But it is bigger than ever the dire wolf was. Perhaps it is the monster of our dreams, when we huddled in caves. Perhaps it was simply a wolf, but we were smaller, little hominids who could never run fast enough to get away.'

Shadow leaned against the rock face behind him. He squeezed his left arm with his right hand to try to stop the bleeding. 'This is Wod's Hill,' said Shadow. 'And that's Wod's dog. I wouldn't put it past him.'

'It doesn't matter.' More stones were placed on stones.

'Ollie,' said Shadow. 'The beast is going to kill you. It's already inside you. It's not a good thing.'

'Old Shuck's not going to hurt me. Old Shuck loves me. Cassie's in the wall,' said Oliver, and he dropped a rock on top of the others with a crash. 'Now you are in the wall with her. Nobody's waiting for you. Nobody's going to come looking for you. Nobody is going to cry for you. Nobody's going to miss you.'

There were, Shadow knew, although he could never have told a soul how he knew, three of them, not two, in that tiny space. There was Cassie Burglass, there in body (rotted and dried and still stinking of decay) and there in soul, and there was also something else, something that twined about his legs, and then butted gently at his injured hand. A voice spoke to him, from somewhere close. He knew that voice, although the accent was unfamiliar.

It was the voice that a cat would speak in, if a cat were a woman: expressive, dark, musical. The voice said, *You should not be here, Shadow. You have to stop, and you must take action. You are letting the rest of the world make your decisions for you.*

Shadow said aloud, 'That's not entirely fair, Bast.'

'You have to be quiet,' said Oliver, gently. 'I mean it.' The stones of the wall were being replaced rapidly and efficiently. Already they were up to Shadow's chest.

Mrr. No? Sweet thing, you really have no idea. No idea who you are or what you are or what that means. If he walls you up in here to die in this hill, this temple will stand forever – and whatever hodgepodge of belief these locals have will work for them and will make magic. But the sun will still go down on them, and all the skies will be grey. All things will mourn, and they will not know what they are mourning for. The world will be worse – for people, for cats, for the remembered, for the forgotten. You have died and you have returned. You matter, Shadow, and you must not meet your death here, a sad sacrifice hidden in a hillside.

'So what are you suggesting I do?' he whispered.

Fight. The Beast is a thing of mind. It's taking its power from you, Shadow. You are near, and so it's become more real. Real enough to own Oliver. Real enough to hurt you.

'Me?'

'You think ghosts can talk to everyone?' asked Cassie Burglass's voice in the darkness, urgently. 'We are moths. And you are the flame.'

'What should I do?' asked Shadow. 'It hurt my arm. It damn near ripped out my throat.'

Oh, sweet man. It's just a shadow-thing. It's a night-dog. It's just an overgrown jackal.

'It's real,' Shadow said. The last of the stones was being banged into place.

'Are you truly scared of your father's dog?' said a woman's voice. Goddess or ghost, Shadow did not know.

But he knew the answer. Yes. Yes, he was scared.

His left arm was only pain, and unusable, and his right hand was slick and sticky with his blood. He was entombed in a cavity between a wall and rock. But he was, for now, alive.

'Get your shit together,' said Cassie. 'I've done everything I can. Do it.'

He braced himself against the rocks behind the wall, and he raised his feet. Then he kicked both his booted feet out together, as hard as he could. He had walked so many miles in the last few months. He was a big man, and he was stronger than most. He put everything he had behind that kick.

The wall exploded.

The Beast was on him, the black dog of despair, but this time Shadow was prepared for it. This time he was the aggressor. He grabbed at it.

I will not be my father's dog.

With his right hand he held the beast's jaw closed. He stared into its green eyes. He did not believe the beast was a dog at all, not really.

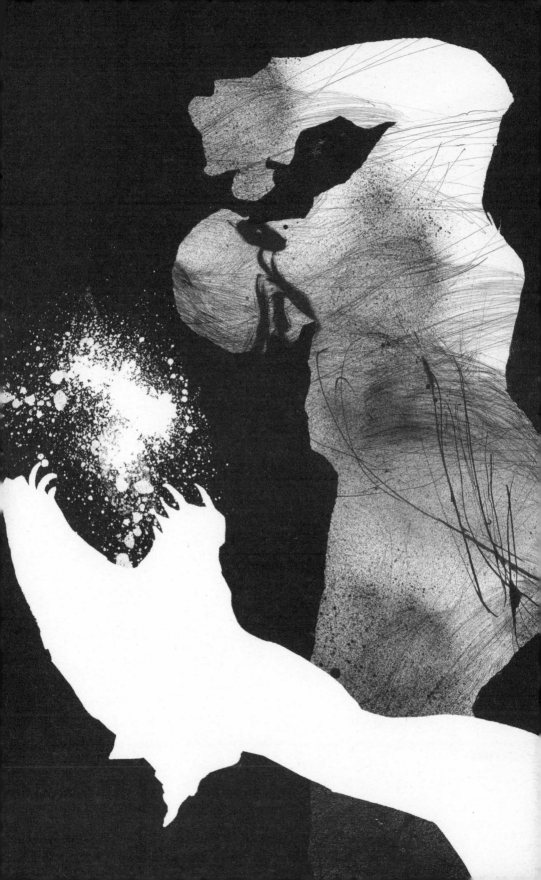

It's daylight, said Shadow to the dog, with his mind, not with his voice. *Run away. Whatever you are, run away. Run back to your gibbet, run back to your grave, little wish hound. All you can do is depress us, fill the world with shadows and illusions. The age when you ran with the Wild Hunt, or hunted terrified humans, it's over. I don't know if you're my father's dog or not. But you know what? I don't care.*

With that, Shadow took a deep breath and let go of the dog's muzzle.

It did not attack. It made a noise, a baffled whine deep in its throat that was almost a whimper.

'Go home,' said Shadow, aloud.

The dog hesitated. Shadow thought for a moment then that he had won, that he was safe, that the dog would simply go away. But then the creature lowered its head, raised the ruff around its neck, and bared its teeth. It would not leave, Shadow knew, until he was dead.

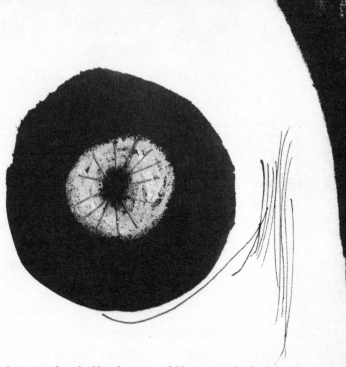

The corridor in the hillside was filling with light: the rising sun shone directly into it. Shadow wondered if the people who had built it, so long ago, had aligned their temple to the sunrise. He took a step to the side, stumbled on something, and fell awkwardly to the ground.

Beside Shadow on the grass was Oliver, sprawled and unconscious. Shadow had tripped over his leg. The man's eyes were closed; he made a growling sound in the back of his throat, and Shadow heard the same sound, magnified and triumphant, from the dark beast that filled the mouth of the temple.

Shadow was down, and hurt, and was, he knew, a dead man.

Something soft touched his face, gently.

Something else brushed his hand. Shadow glanced to his side, and he understood. He understood why Bast had been with him in this place, and he understood who had brought her.

They had been ground up and sprinkled on these fields more than a hundred years before, stolen from the earth around the temple of Bastet and Beni Hasan. Tons upon tons of them, mummified cats in their thousands, each cat a tiny representation of the deity, each cat an act of worship preserved for an eternity.

They were there, in that space, beside him: brown and sand coloured and shadowy grey, cats with leopard spots and cats with tiger stripes, wild, lithe and ancient. These were not the local cats Bast had sent to watch him the previous day. These were the ancestors of those cats, of all our modern cats, from Egypt, from the Nile Delta, from thousands of years ago, brought here to make things grow.

They trilled and chirrupped, they did not meow.

The black dog growled louder but now it made no move to attack. Shadow forced himself into a sitting position. 'I thought I told you to go home, Shuck,' he said.

The dog did not move. Shadow opened his right hand, and gestured. It was a gesture of dismissal, of impatience. *Finish this.*

The cats sprang, with ease, as if choreographed. They landed on the beast, each of them a coiled spring of fangs and claws, both as sharp as they had ever been in life. Pin-sharp claws sank into the black flanks of the huge beast, tore at its eyes. It snapped at them, angrily, and pushed itself against the wall, toppling more rocks, in an attempt to shake them off, but without success. Angry teeth sank into its ears, its muzzle, its tail, its paws.

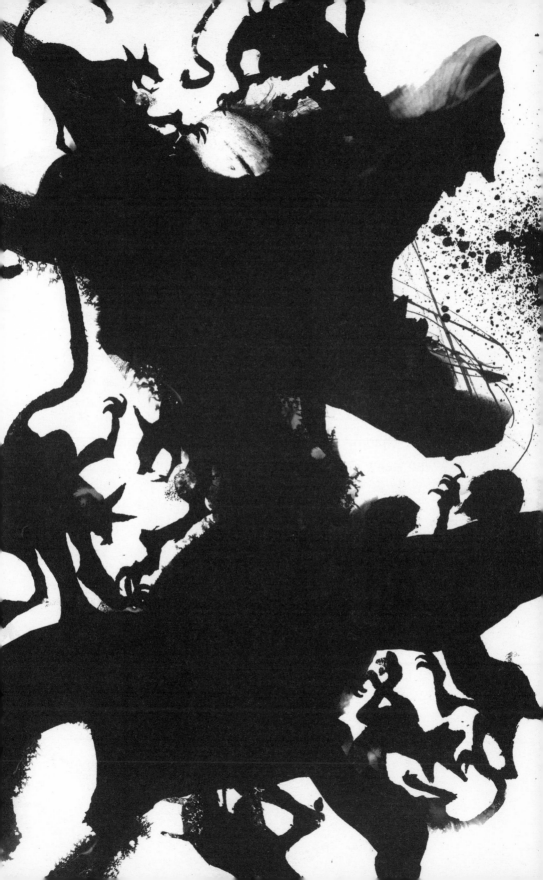

The beast yelped and growled, and then it made a noise which, Shadow thought, would, had it come from any human throat, have been a scream.

Shadow was never certain what happened then. He watched the black dog put its muzzle down to Oliver's mouth, and push, hard. He could have sworn that the creature stepped *into* Oliver, like a bear stepping into a river.

Oliver shook, violently, on the sand.

The scream faded, and the beast was gone, and sunlight filled the space on the hill.

Shadow felt himself shivering. He felt like he had just woken up from a waking sleep; emotions flooded through him, like sunlight: fear and revulsion and grief and hurt, deep hurt.

There was anger in there, too. Oliver had tried to kill him, he knew, and he was thinking clearly for the first time in days.

A man's voice shouted, 'Hold up! Everyone all right over there?'

A high bark, and a lurcher ran in, sniffed at Shadow, his back against the wall, sniffed at Oliver Bierce, unconscious on the ground, and at the remains of Cassie Burglass.

A man's silhouette filled the opening to the outside world, a grey paper cutout against the rising sun.

'Needles! Leave it!' he said. The dog returned to the man's side. The man said, 'I heard someone screaming. Leastways, I wouldn't swear to it being a someone. But I heard it. Was that you?'

And then he saw the body, and he stopped. 'Holy fucking mother of all fucking bastards,' he said.

'Her name was Cassie Burglass,' said Shadow.

'Moira's old girlfriend?' said the man. Shadow knew him as the landlord of the pub, could not remember whether he had ever known the man's name. 'Bloody Nora. I thought she went to London.'

Shadow felt sick.

The landlord was kneeling beside Oliver. 'His heart's still beating,' he said. 'What happened to him?'

'I'm not sure,' said Shadow. 'He screamed when he saw the body – you must have heard him. Then he just went down. And your dog came in.'

The man looked at Shadow, worried. 'And you? Look at you! What happened to you, man?'

'Oliver asked me to come up here with him. Said he had something awful he had to get off his chest.' Shadow looked at the wall on each side of the corridor. There were other bricked-in nooks there. Shadow had a good idea of what would be found behind them if any of them were opened. 'He asked me to help him open the wall. I did. He knocked me over as he went down. Took me by surprise.'

'Did he tell you why he had done it?'

'Jealousy,' said Shadow. 'Just jealous of Moira and Cassie, even after Moira had left Cassie for him.'

The man exhaled, shook his head. 'Bloody hell,' he said. 'Last bugger I'd expect to do anything like this. Needles! Leave it!' He pulled a mobile phone from his pocket, and called the police. Then he excused himself. 'I've got a bag of game to put aside until the police have cleared out,' he explained.

Shadow got to his feet, and inspected his arms. His sweater and coat were both ripped in the left arm, as if by huge teeth, but his skin was unbroken beneath it. There was no blood on his clothes, no blood on his hands.

He wondered what his corpse would have looked like, if the black dog had killed him.

Cassie's ghost stood beside him, and looked down at her body, half-fallen from the hole in the wall. The corpse's fingertips and the fingernails were wrecked, Shadow observed, as if she had tried, in the hours or the days before she died, to dislodge the rocks of the wall.

'Look at that,' she said, staring at herself. 'Poor thing. Like a cat in a glass box.' Then she turned to Shadow. 'I didn't actually fancy you,' she said. 'Not even a little bit. I'm not sorry. I just needed to get your attention.'

'I know,' said Shadow. 'I just wish I'd met you when you were alive. We could have been friends.'

'I bet we would have been. It was hard in there. It's good to be done with all of this. And I'm sorry, Mr American. Try not to hate me.'

Shadow's eyes were watering. He wiped his eyes on his shirt. When he looked again, he was alone in the passageway.

'I don't hate you,' he told her.

He felt a hand squeeze his hand. He walked outside, into the morning sunlight, and he breathed and shivered, and listened to the distant sirens.

Two men arrived and carried Oliver off on a stretcher, down the hill to the road where an ambulance took him away, siren screaming to alert any sheep on the lanes that they should shuffle back to the grass verge.

A female police officer turned up as the ambulance disappeared, accompanied by a younger male officer. They knew the landlord, whom Shadow was not surprised to learn was also a Scathelocke, and were both impressed by Cassie's remains, to the point that the young male officer left the passageway and vomited into the ferns.

If it occurred to either of them to inspect the other bricked-in cavities in the corridor, for evidence of centuries-old crimes, they managed to suppress the idea, and Shadow was not going to suggest it.

He gave them a brief statement, then rode with them to the local police station, where he gave a fuller statement to a large police officer with a serious beard. The officer appeared mostly concerned that Shadow was provided with a mug of instant coffee, and that Shadow, as an American tourist, would not form a mistaken impression of rural England. 'It's not like this up here normally. It's really quiet. Lovely place. I wouldn't want you to think we were all like this.'

Shadow assured him that he didn't think that at all.

VI

THE RIDDLE

Moira was waiting for him when he came out of the police station. She was standing with a woman in her early sixties, who looked comfortable and reassuring, the sort of person you would want at your side in a crisis.

'Shadow, this is Doreen. My sister.'

Doreen shook hands, explaining she was sorry she hadn't been able to be there during the last week, but she had been moving house.

'Doreen's a county court judge,' explained Moira.

Shadow could not easily imagine this woman as a judge.

'They are waiting for Ollie to come around,' said Moira. 'Then they are going to charge him with murder.' She said it thoughtfully, but in the same way she would have asked Shadow where he thought she ought to plant some snapdragons.

'And what are you going to do?'

She scratched her nose. 'I'm in shock. I have no idea what I'm doing any more. I keep thinking about the last few years. Poor, poor Cassie. She never thought there was any malice in him.'

'I never liked him,' said Doreen, and she sniffed. 'Too full of facts for my liking, and he never knew when to stop talking. Just kept wittering on. Like he was trying to cover something up.'

'Your backpack and your laundry are in Doreen's car,' said Moira. 'I thought we could give you a lift somewhere, if you needed one. Or if you want to get back to rambling, you can walk.'

'Thank you,' said Shadow. He knew he would never be welcome in Moira's little house, not any more.

Moira said, urgently, angrily, as if it was all she wanted to know, 'You said you saw Cassie. You *told* us, yesterday. That was what sent Ollie off the deep end. It hurt me so much. Why did you say you'd seen her, if she was dead? You *couldn't* have seen her.'

Shadow had been wondering about that, while he had been giving his police statement. 'Beats me,' he said. 'I don't believe in ghosts. Probably a local, playing some kind of game with the Yankee tourist.'

Moira looked at him with fierce hazel eyes, as if she was trying to believe him but was unable to make the final leap of faith. Her sister reached down and held her hand. 'More things in heaven and earth, Horatio. I think we should just leave it at that.'

Moira looked at Shadow, unbelieving, angered, for a long time, before she took a deep breath and said, 'Yes. Yes, I suppose we should.'

There was silence in the car. Shadow wanted to apologise to Moira, to say something that would make things better.

They drove past the gibbet tree.

'There were ten tongues within one head,' recited Doreen, in a voice slightly higher and more formal than the one in which she had previously spoken. *'And one went out to fetch some bread, to feed the living and the dead.* That was a riddle written about this corner, and that tree.'

'What does it mean?'

'A wren made a nest inside the skull of a gibbeted corpse, flying in and out of the jaw to feed its young. In the midst of death, as it were, life just keeps on happening.'

Shadow thought about the matter for a little while, and told her that he guessed that it probably did.

NEIL GAIMAN
AMERICAN GODS

Would you believe
that all the gods that
people have ever imagined
are still with us today?

Available now from

HEADLINE

NEIL GAIMAN

ANANSI BOYS

Anansi was a spider, when the world was young,
and all the stories were being told for the first time.
He used to get himself into trouble, and he used to
get himself out of trouble. The story of the
tar-baby, the one they tell about Brer Rabbit?
That was Anansi's story first. Some people think
he was a rabbit. But that's their mistake.
He wasn't a rabbit. He was a spider.

Available now from

HEADLINE

NEIL GAIMAN

THE MONARCH OF THE GLEN

Everything seemed sharp and
jutting, even the grey clouds that
scudded across the pale blue sky.
It was as if the bones of the
world showed through.

Available now from

HEADLINE